LITTLE BABY MONSTER

WRITTEN AND ILLUSTRATED BY
ZACHARY SCOTT HEINRICHS

TO MY MOM

FROM YOUR
LITTLE BABY MONSTER

GOOD MORNING LITTLE BABY MONSTER!

IT'S TIME TO WAKE UP!

LITTLE BABY MONSTER LOVES TO PLAY.

LITTLE BABY MONSTER MAKES A MESS ALL DAY.

LITTLE BABY MONSTER LOVES TO EAT.

LITTLE BABY MONSTER EATS SOME SWEETS.

LITTLE BABY MONSTER LOVES TO SWING.

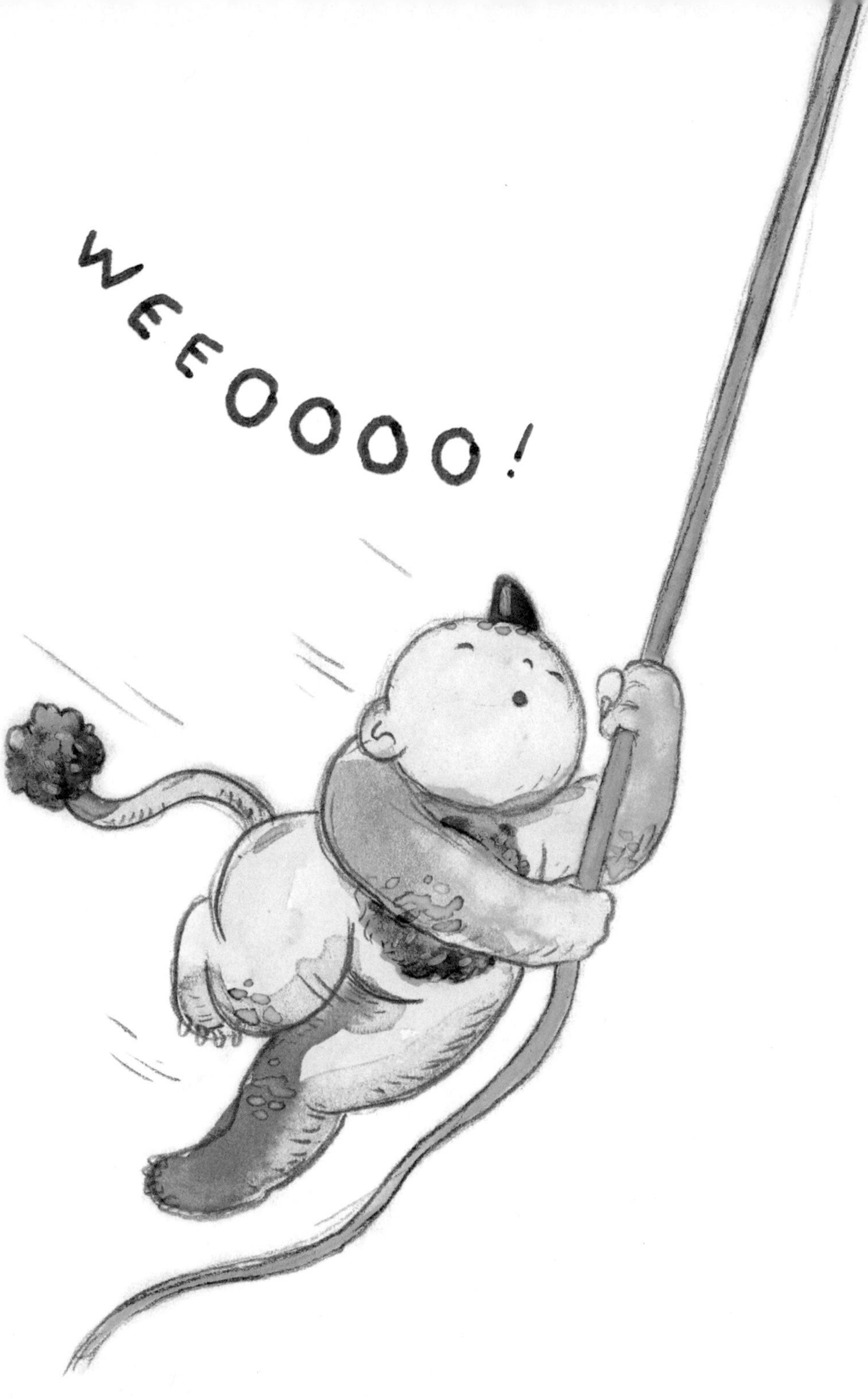
WEEOOOO!

HE LOVES TO DANCE.

HE LOVES TO SING.

HE LOVES TO SHARE HIS LITTLE BEAR.

HE LOVES TO LAUGH.

HE LOVES TO CARE.

SOMETIMES HE'S SCARED.

SOMETIMES HE'S SAD.

SOMETIMES HE'S JUST REALLY BAD.

BUT WE STILL LOVE HIM.

AND HE LOVES US TOO.

AND HE'LL ALWAYS BE THERE.

FOR ME AND FOR YOU.

SO WHEN THE DAY IS DONE AND IT'S TIME TO REST,

HE DOES THE THING HE LOVES THE BEST.

GOODNIGHT LITTLE BABY MONSTER.

ZACHARY SCOTT HEINRICHS IS AN ARTIST, WRITER, AND MUSICIAN WITH A WILD IMAGINATION. HE GREW UP IN MENIFEE, CALIFORNIA WITH HIS BROTHER JESSE AND HIS DOGS LUCKY, ROWDY, AND RASCAL. THEY WERE REALLY GOOD DOGS. HE ENJOYS READING, LISTENING TO MUSIC, AND WATCHING MOVIES WITH HIS FRIENDS. THIS IS ZACH'S FIRST CHILDREN'S BOOK.

EMAIL: MANWIZARDS@GMAIL.COM

Made in the USA
Las Vegas, NV
09 July 2022

51289452R00031